Beautiful
Beautiful
Bird

Lisa Coriale

Illustrated by Stephen Adams

AuthorHouse™ LLC
1663 Liberty Drive
Bloomington, IN 47403
www.authorhouse.com
Phone: 1-800-839-8640

Published by AuthorHouse 07/16/2014

ISBN: 978-1-4969-1998-4 (sc)
978-1-4969-1997-7 (e)

Library of Congress Control Number: 2014911327

Any people depicted in stock imagery provided by Thinkstock are models,
and such images are being used for illustrative purposes only.
Certain stock imagery © Thinkstock.

This book is printed on acid-free paper.

authorHOUSE®

Dedicated to Milla, Kristian, Nico, Carmen, Skyla and Leo.
And all of my loving family.

About the Author

Lisa Coriale has recently completed a Bachelor of Journalism Degree with a certificate in Aboriginal Studies. She also holds a Bachelor of Social Work degree.

Lisa has spent the last few years as a member of the Kamloops Mayors Advisory Committee for peoples with disabilities. She has a passion to advocate for people with disabilities. She wants people with disabilities to be seen as individuals with much to offer the rest of their communities.

Lisa lives with her parents in Kamloops, BC. She was diagnosed with Quadripelegic Cerebral Palsy as a small child. This has not slowed her down. She does not let her disability interfere with her hopes and dreams. Lisa is an amazing young woman with a heart as large as her talents. Lisa plans on writing articles for newspapers and magazines as well as short stories and an autobiography

Beautiful Beautiful Bird

Published 2008, in Transparent

Author Lisa Coriale

Beautiful, Beautiful Bird

You are the sparkle of my eye

Beautiful, beautiful bird

I gave you wings to fly

So don't be afraid,

You beautiful bird

I am here to help you

So spread your wings,

You beautiful bird

I created you to soar

So you must fly,

You beautiful bird

Once upon a time there was a family of talented birds.

Their feathers were very bright and colourful like a rainbow.

There was a mama bird and papa bird. They had four little birds.

Their names were: Lucy, Gabe, Bella and Nikki.

The smallest bird was different in two ways.

She had a broken wing and she could not sing very well.

She wanted to sing like all the other birds of the forest.

They sounded so beautiful.

Where the bird family lived, the sun was always shining

and the flowers were blooming.

The grass was thick and fun to play in for the little birds.

Sometimes Nikki got hurt and Lucy, Gabe and Bella would come and bandage her up.

The mama bird was wise and she kept her children close.

The papa bird did very well at providing for his family.

Each of the chicks had a special gift. The two sisters loved to sing and dance and the brother liked to build things. The littlest bird did not know what her gift was yet. She wanted to find out.

Both the mama bird and the papa bird encouraged their chicks to follow their dreams.

The bird family went on many adventures. They crossed streams and the mama bird always told Nikki, the beautiful bird, to always try to do things in a different way because of her broken wing.

When the littlest bird felt sad and alone she would go to a special place where the sun was always shining down upon her. It made her feel all warm and fuzzy inside.

Sometimes she would be sad about her broken wing because she could not fly.

The sun would remind her how beautiful she was.

The sun told her that she had treasures inside and to share those treasures

with all the animals of the forest.

The sun had one more thing to tell the beautiful bird. Even though she did not have a good singing voice, she could use her voice to tell everyone her story. The beautiful bird realized that this was her special gift. She did not have to fly to use it.

She was very excited to tell her family that she found out what her special gift was.

The next day, all the animals of the forest came to see and hear the beautiful bird. She told them what the sun had said.

The sun shone down upon her in an extra special way that day. Her feathers were as bright as a rainbow in the sky. The beautiful bird was shining from the inside out.

All of the animals of the forest took what the beautiful bird had to say in their hearts.

The beautiful bird's family was very proud of her and the sun continued to shine upon her from that day forward.

THE END

CPSIA information can be obtained at www.ICGtesting.com
Printed in the USA
LVOW05s1241090615

441725LV00002B/3/P